OTHER YEARLING BOOKS YOU WILL ENJOY:

Miss Clafooty and the Demon, J. DAVID TOWNSEND

The Strange Story of the Frog Who Became a Prince
ELINOR LANDER HORWITZ

The Smartest Bear and His Brother Oliver, ALICE BACH

A Toad for Tuesday, RUSSELL E. ERICKSON

Headlines, MALCOLM HALL

Maybe, A Mole, JULIA CUNNINGHAM

The Case of the Elevator Duck, POLLY BERRIEN BERENDS

The Clay Pot Boy, CYNTHIA JAMESON

The Carp in the Bathtub, BARBARA COHEN

Once Under the Cherry Blossom Tree, ALLEN SAY

YEARLING BOOKS are designed especially to entertain and enlighten young people. The finest available books for children have been selected under the direction of Charles F. Reasoner, Professor of Elementary Education, New York University.

For a complete listing of all Yearling titles,
write to Education Sales Department, Dell Publishing Co., Inc.,
1 Dag Hammarskjold Plaza, New York, N.Y. 10017

The Witch's Egg

by **MADELEINE EDMONDSON**

illustrated by **KAY CHORAO**

A Yearling Book

Published by
Dell Publishing Co., Inc.
1 Dag Hammarskjold Plaza
New York, New York 10017

Yearling ® TM 913705, Dell Publishing Co., Inc.

ISBN: 0-440-49476-1

Reprinted by arrangement with The Seabury Press, Inc.

Printed in the United States of America
Third Dell Printing—March 1978

for Nelly and Daisy

AGATHA was an old, old, bad-tempered witch. She had a pointed nose and mean little eyes. She wore a long black dress, black lace-up boots, and a tall black hat, and she rode through the sky on a broomstick.

Agatha made her home on top of Lost Mountain in an empty nest that an eagle had built long ago and then abandoned. She lived all alone, because she had no friends. She had never had any.

An eagle's nest is not a very comfortable place to live, but Agatha didn't care. She never bothered to fix it up.

Her only piece of furniture was a small portable television set. She liked to watch horror movies on it. The only other things she owned were her comfortable bedroom slippers, the broom she rode on, and a black shawl with fringe all around it.

Most of the day Agatha slept curled up in the nest, covered by her shawl. At night she would fly into town on her broom, to begin her night's work of scaring people.

Agatha would fly up close to the windows of houses and look in; then she would bump and thump against the glass and fly away.

Sometimes she would bang on a door and then fly off before anyone could answer. Or she would follow some person who was walking alone down a dark empty street and fly right over his head, so he could feel a cold draft on the back of his neck.

She would fly to the roof of a house and stamp her feet—or look down the chimney and laugh in a horrid, cackling, frightening manner. She was very good at her work. After all, she had been practicing for hundreds of years.

One night while Agatha was in town, hard at work frightening the townspeople, a cuckoo came to the eagle's nest. Cuckoos always lay their eggs in other birds' nests because they are too lazy to build nests of their own and bring up their babies themselves.

This mother cuckoo thought she had found an especially nice place right on top of Agatha's black shawl, so she laid her egg there. Then she flew away, very pleased with herself for being such a good mother.

When Agatha came back from work, she took off her tight pointed black boots and put on her comfortable old slippers. Then she looked around for her shawl and saw the egg lying on it.

"What's this?" she cried. "What is this nasty egg doing on my shawl? And where's the unmannerly bird who laid it?"

She hunted everywhere in the eagle's nest to see if a mother bird was hiding there. "Come out, you!" she scolded. "Come out of wherever you are and take your disgusting egg away from my nest!" But of course she could not find the mother bird.

Agatha was so angry that she climbed onto her broom and flew from tree to tree asking all the mother birds on Lost Mountain if they knew who had left the egg in her nest.

The birds had always been afraid of Agatha because she looked so mean and never spoke to any of them, but they were very much interested in the egg she had found. They all flew back to the eagle's nest with her to have a look at it. None of them could tell what kind of bird it belonged to, but they all agreed that it should not stay in Agatha's nest.

"If that egg isn't kept warm, it will never hatch," a robin pointed out.

"That's right," agreed a thrush. "Someone must sit on it and keep it warm till it hatches. It's the only way."

"Yes," cried all the mother birds. "That's what must be done. Give it to one of us and we will keep it nice and warm and hatch it with our own eggs. We'll give it a good start in life."

"It's such a big, handsome egg, too," said a sparrow. "I'd be proud to have it in my nest."

As soon as Agatha realized that all the birds wanted the egg for their own, she decided to keep it. "Go away, all you silly birds," she said. "This egg is mine. You all admit you don't know who left it here, and I found it in my nest. Finders keepers."

"But you don't know how to hatch it," twittered the birds.

"Hatching it will be simple," said Agatha. "Witches are clever and birds are stupid. If a bird can hatch an egg, a witch can hatch it better."

So Agatha gave up work for days and days and stayed in the nest keeping the egg warm. She held it carefully on her lap, nicely covered by her black shawl. Every day the mother birds came to ask if she wanted to change her mind and give the egg to them. She told them to go back and sit on their own eggs.

Agatha watched old movies on her television set at night and slept during the day, and the time went very, very slowly. She was bored and uncomfortable, but she would not give up. She was determined that she was going to hatch the egg. She began to wonder what kind of bird would come out of it. Perhaps it would turn out to be something special.

At last, on the thirteenth day, she heard the sound of a little beak chipping away inside the eggshell. And out came the baby cuckoo.

He was very ugly. He didn't have any feathers yet and his eyes were still shut. But from the very first minute his mouth was open, waiting for someone to put food in it. Agatha had never looked at a baby bird before, but she could tell this one was hungry and she looked around for something to feed it.

Agatha herself had always lived on chocolate sandwich cookies and ginger ale. That was what she liked best; besides, it really doesn't matter what witches eat, because they live forever anyway and never get sick. So she started feeding the baby bird on cookie crumbs.

When the mother birds arrived for their daily visit, they were shocked to see what was going on. They told Agatha exactly what they thought of such an unbalanced diet.

"He's such a beautiful baby," they chirped. "Look at that big yellow beak! See those strong little pin-feathers! But you can't feed him that stuff!"

"Worms," the robin said. "He must have lots of worms to make his bones grow strong."

"And bugs," cried the thrush. "Bugs will make his feathers soft and shiny. That's what baby birds eat."

"My bird eats whatever I give him," said Agatha. "This is no ordinary common bird. This bird is mine and his name is Witchbird. Go back to your nests and don't bother us."

But Agatha knew that the mother birds were right about what baby birds should eat, so secretly she went out to catch insects for Witchbird. Insects are hard to catch, and Agatha did her hunting in the dark while the mother birds were asleep, which made it even harder.

Sometimes Agatha grumbled to herself as she chased after bugs with a little flashlight and butterfly net, but soon she found that she didn't really mind all the extra work. She was glad to do it because she was so pleased with the way she was bringing up Witchbird. She knew she was taking better care of him than any silly bird could ever hope to do.

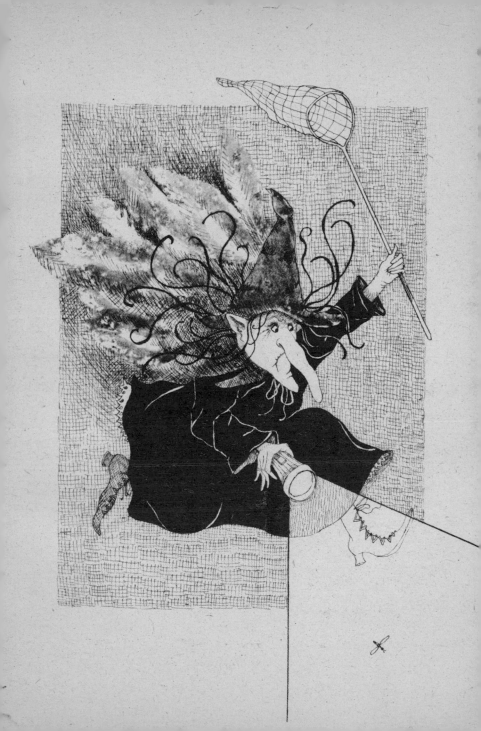

Agatha was proud of how big and strong Witchbird was getting, and she was prouder still of how clever he was. Very soon he learned to talk, and then she began to teach him all the secrets witches know. Every night, instead of going into town to work, she stayed in the nest and gave Witchbird his lessons.

Agatha had forgotten how interesting the old witch stories were. She enjoyed telling Witchbird all about the lives of the great witches of olden days. Soon he knew the whole history of witchcraft almost as well as she did. But Witchbird's favorite story was always the one about how he was hatched from the egg.

"Tell me the story again, Agatha," he would ask.

"What story?" Agatha would answer, though she knew perfectly well what story he wanted.

"The one about how you found the egg, and how all the mother birds came and wanted it but you decided to hatch it instead. And how you waited and waited—"

"And then what happened?" Agatha teased.

"Oh, don't you remember, Agatha? On the thirteenth day you heard the sound of a tiny beak chipping away inside the egg—and it was me!"·

"Yes," Agatha said. "It certainly did turn out to be you. All right, Witchbird, you sit down and fold your wings nicely and I'll tell you the whole story from the very beginning."

When Witchbird grew old enough to leave the nest, Agatha gave him flying lessons, too. They practiced flying all around Lost Mountain, and when Witchbird was tired he would perch on Agatha's broomstick and ride with her. Then Agatha would take him back to the nest and leave him there to rest while she went off to work.

But Witchbird didn't like to be left alone. "Stay with me, Agatha," he would say. "Tell me a story."

"No," said Agatha, shaking her head. "I'd like to stay with you, but I have work to do. I must not neglect my duty."

"Then why not take me with you?" Witchbird asked. "Couldn't I help you work? Couldn't I learn to scare people?"

"Of course not," said Agatha. "You're too young. You stay here in the nest and wait for me. I'll be back in the morning."

But as she flew about the town, Agatha began to wonder. Perhaps Witchbird could help her, after all. Perhaps they could do frightening things together that she could never do alone. And besides, if Witchbird came to work with her, he wouldn't have to be lonely all night while he waited for her to come home.

So Agatha trained Witchbird to help her with her work. Every night they flew to the nearby town looking for people to frighten. Agatha and Witchbird would fly up to the windows of houses and knock on them. Witchbird would knock with his beak. Then the two of them would be off, down a dark street to look for someone walking alone. Together they could make a wonderful draft, Agatha with her broom, Witchbird with his flapping wings. Agatha taught Witchbird a terrifying cackle, and to hear the two of them laughing together was enough to make a person's hair stand on end with fright.

Agatha was happy at last. She had never been really happy in her life before, and now she knew why. It was because she had never had a friend before. Having Witchbird with her made everything pleasant. Scaring people wasn't just work any more: it was fun now, because they did it together.

All through the summer and early fall, Agatha and Witchbird lived the lives of happy witches. By day they slept and by night they swooped about doing their witchy tricks. But as the leaves changed from green to yellow and red and then to brown, and started to fall from the trees, things began to change. Witchbird was not the same. He didn't ask Agatha to tell him the old witch stories in the evening. He didn't even ask for his own story. He was too quiet.

Agatha could see that he was unhappy, and she worried about it. At last she decided that she had to find out what the matter was.

"I can see you have something on your mind, Witchbird," she said one morning, "and you must tell me what it is. I hatched you from the egg. I am your best friend. I have a right to know."

"All right, Agatha," said Witchbird, "I'll tell you. I see all the other birds flying south and I . . . I want to fly with them."

"You must be joking!" cried Agatha. "You mean you want to go south with those silly birds? You want to be with them instead of with *me*?"

"I know you are my best friend, Agatha," said Witchbird, hanging his head. "And I will always be grateful that you hatched me from the egg. But the life we live is not the life for me."

"But Witchbird," Agatha protested, "we live the way all witches do. We have a wonderful life."

"It is a wonderful life for a witch," said Witchbird,
"but I'm not really a witch, you know. I'm a bird,
and all the birds are flying south."

Agatha was very sad. Now that she was used to having Witchbird living with her, she didn't see how she could live alone. There would be nobody to talk to, nobody to tell stories to, nobody to fly with.

"No, Witchbird," she said. "You can't go."

"I must, Agatha. I can't help it," Witchbird said. "But I will never forget you. I will always think of you as my best friend."

Agatha watched as Witchbird flew over Lost Mountain, heading toward the south. As he flew past the tallest pine tree he looked back, and Agatha waved. With the corner of her black shawl she wiped away the first tear she had ever shed.

It was a long, hard winter for Agatha. She missed Witchbird terribly. The snow fell and the wind howled and Agatha went on as usual. Witches don't feel the cold, and Agatha could sit in the eagle's nest and watch old horror movies on her TV even with an icicle hanging from the end of her nose. And every night, in hail or snow or sleet or bitter cold, she flew through the town doing her witch's work. But she was a very lonely old witch.

At last the long, cold winter came to an end and spring began. Little by little the snow melted. The ice broke up and floated down the stream, and the first crocuses began to push out of the ground. Leaf buds formed on the trees.

Agatha tried not to notice any of these things, but she knew that all the birds had come back to Lost Mountain. In almost every tree a nest was being built, ready for the new families the mother birds would soon begin to raise.

One day the mother birds came to visit Agatha. They perched all around the edge of the eagle's nest.

"We've come to tell you the news about Witchbird, Agatha," said the robin importantly.

"I'm the one who saw him," said the chickadee, all excited. "I'm the one who saw him, not you."

"Witchbird is in Florida," went on the robin, who never paid any attention to chickadees. "He's living in an orange grove there, and he's as happy as a lark."

"We knew you'd want to hear all about it," said the woodpecker. "Especially since you and he used to be such good friends."

"I'm the one who talked to him, and I'm the only one who knows exactly what he said," cried the chickadee. "Witchbird told me all about his future plans. He's going to live in the orange grove for the rest of his days and—"

"We knew you must be worrying about him night and day," interrupted the thrush. "That's why we came. Now you needn't worry about Witchbird any more."

"I never do," snapped Agatha. "To tell the truth, I never think about him at all. I can't even remember what he looks like."

"Well," said the thrush, "we can certainly understand how lonely you must be, all by yourself here with nobody to keep you company."

"And that's why we're going to come and visit you every day, Agatha," the robin went on. "We've decided that it's our duty to cheer you up."

"No!" shouted Agatha. "No! I don't want you to cheer me up. Don't you silly creatures know that birds of a feather may flock together but witches enjoy being alone? Now go back to your nests and stay there. Forever, please."

The mother birds flew angrily away and Agatha was glad she had seen the last of them. She did not want to be reminded of Witchbird. She wanted to forget about him and concentrate on her work. And that is just what she did. She worked every night until she was exhausted. She slept every day until it was time to work again.

Then one evening, just as the sun was setting, Agatha was awakened suddenly from her day's sleep by a great rustle and flapping of wings. Something had landed on the edge of the eagle's nest. She threw off her shawl and sat up—and there on the edge of the nest was a bird. In its beak it was holding a spray of orange blossoms. It was Witchbird himself.

"I had to come back, Agatha," he said. "I've brought you these flowers all the way from Florida. I thought I would settle down and live there forever, but I couldn't do it. I missed you."

Agatha thought she might be dreaming. She had sometimes had dreams like this during the long winter. Then she took the orange blossoms and smelled them. She decided she was awake.

So that's the way Agatha and Witchbird live now.
Every fall he flies off to Florida with the other birds.
And every spring he comes back to the big nest on
Lost Mountain and his friend Agatha.

Every night, all summer long, they fly through the
town together, thumping, bumping, cackling, and
scaring people out of their wits. If you are walking
alone down a dark street some summer night, and
suddenly you feel a cold draft on the back of your
neck, look up quickly. Perhaps you will see Agatha
and Witchbird flying past.